Little Dune

Lisa Van der Wielen

Illustrated by Alison Mutton

For my daughter, Mia:
Let the tide wash your worries away.
-LW

About the Author

Lisa Van Der Wielen is a primary school teacher and writer from Perth, Western Australia. Her passions for teaching and writing lead her to become a Children's Author in 2017. Her love for the beach, nature, dogs, family and the importance of virtues provide her with motivation to write poetry and stories that inspire. Her books proudly support the charities Perth Children's Hospital and Ronald McDonald House Perth.

Lisa Van Der Wielen is the author of:
Vegetarian Polony | Luna Lucy | Aqua Dog | The Life of Gus |
Luna Lucy and the Planets | Aqua Dog Flames | Little Dune

About the Illustrator

Alison Mutton is an illustrator from Perth, Western Australia. She graduated from Curtin University with a Bachelor of Design (Hons) majoring in Illustration, in 2008 and has been working in the children's and educational publishing fields ever since. When not illustrating and designing, she enjoys walking her dog Myrna, playing the piano, needle felting and swing dancing. Among her other titles, she has previously illustrated *Aqua Dog* and *Aqua Dog Flames* for Lisa Van Der Wielen.

Little Dune

First published February 2022
Hardback: ISBN 978-0-6453979-1-8 Paperback: ISBN 978-0-6453979-2-5

Text © Lisa Van Der Wielen 2022
Illustrations © Alison Mutton / Alene Illustration 2022

The moral rights of the author and illustrator have been asserted.

Typeset in Duality
Graphic Design: Alison Mutton

Alene Illustration
www.alene-art.com

Grace loved to go to the beach, but she didn't always love to go into the water.

She was scared.

She was frightened of the water and everything that lay beneath.

Grace worried about most things.

She worried about what might happen.
She worried about her family.
She worried about her friends.

Her mum would hold her hand and sing:

"Put your toes in the sand, you will be okay.
Let the ripples of water
wash your worries away.

A wave is a worry, a worry's a wave,
Stand up and face it,
and learn to be brave."

Grace would look down
at her little toes in the soft white sand
and wait for the foamy white waves to reach them.

Part of her wanted
to run backwards, but she also
wanted to feel the cool water on
her feet.

She would wait for
the ocean to take her anxieties
away with the tide.

Sometimes it helped,
but sometimes it didn't.

So, Grace would go and sit
on her towel, watching her family
as they splashed around
in the water.

One hot, sunny day,
Grace and her family went to the beach –

and she heard a soft whimpering sound
coming from behind the sand dunes.

Grace ambled over the grassy banks until the noise became louder.

Curled up in the shade of a tree, looking scared and afraid,
was a scruffy-looking puppy.

Its cute, beady little eyes peered up at Grace
through tufts of wavy fur.

"Hello there, little one,"
Grace said, calmly bending down to pick it up.
"Don't be afraid."

The puppy cuddled into Grace's arms and stopped whining.

With a smile on her face, Grace jogged back to her family, excited and
eager to share her discovery.

"Mum, look what I found in the sand dunes! A little lost puppy. It was
scared and alone. Can we keep it?"

Grace's eyes pleaded
with her mother.

She had always wanted
a dog of her own.

"We had better take the puppy to the vet," her mother said, "and if and only if it doesn't already have a family, we will think about keeping it.

Dogs are a big commitment, Grace," she explained.

"They need feeding and teaching and looking after, just like children."

Grace began to worry.

She worried that she would not be able to keep the puppy.

She worried about whether it would be okay.

But Grace understood her mother's reasoning and helped her
take it to the vet.

The vet checked the puppy all over
and scanned it for a microchip.

"Well, she's a lucky little puppy," the vet said.
"Lucky that you found her. It seems she doesn't have an owner,
but she is healthy. Some food and water and rest, and she'll be
ready to take home."

Grace couldn't believe the puppy was a girl.

She pulled on her mum's arm with excitement and asked, "Can we take her home, Mum? Please?"

Grace's mum smiled and winked. "Maybe we should call her Lucky?"
"Dune," Grace said. "I want to call her Dune."

Dune snuggled into Grace all the way home from the vet.

But before going home,
Grace wanted to stop at the beach where
she'd found her new best friend.

Grace put Dune down near the water's edge.
The puppy immediately hid behind Grace's legs,
afraid of the crashing waves.

Grace bent down and cuddled Dune as she sang:

"Put your paws in the sand, you will be okay.
Let the ripples of water wash your worries away.

A wave is a worry, a worry's a wave,
Stand up and face it
and learn to be brave."

Made in the USA
Coppell, TX
22 February 2022

73958685R00019

Simple Science Experiments
with Elmo and Friends

Water and Earth

By Gina Gold

Illustrated by Tom Brannon

Dover Publications, Inc.
Mineola, New York

Book concept and project supervisor: Jason Schneider

Book design and layout: Ellen Christiansen Kraft

Project editor: Alison Daurio

Sesame Street editor: Pamela Thomas

Bibliographical Note

Sesame Street® Simple Science Experiments with Elmo and Friends: Water and Earth is a new work, first published by Dover Publications, Inc., in 2012.

International Standard Book Number

ISBN-13: 978-0-486-33108-9
ISBN-10: 0-486-33108-3

Manufactured in the United States by Courier Corporation
33108302
www.doverpublications.com